W9-BIM-705

For Wisteria, who knows how to throw a snowball

Dashing Through the Snow

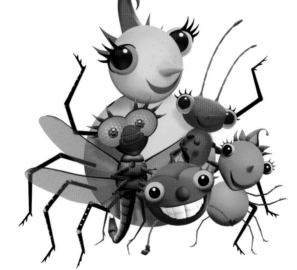

By David Kirk

Callaway

New York 2005

It was a frosty Holly Day in Sunny Patch. Miss Spider, Squirt, and Bounce had been visiting their friend Mrs. Websly.

"Thanks for the holly berry cake!" called Miss Spider as they stepped out into the chilly afternoon air.

"*Sniff sniff!* Can we have some cake right now, Mom? *Please?*" begged Bounce.

"I think we'll save it for after dinner, Bounce," laughed Miss Spider. "Right now, we'd better get crawling so we can get home in time for our family Holly Day feast."

"Look!" yelled Squirt happily. "It's snowing!"

"Yay! *More, more, more* snow!" Bounce cried as he lapped up snowflakes with his tongue.

"Let's not wish for too much snow, boys," Miss Spider warned, "or we won't make it back tonight!"

The boys stopped in their tracks. What if they missed their Holly Day feast?

Squirt had a great idea. "I know how we can get home faster," he said, tugging a big dried leaf out of the snow.

"Hop on, Mom!" laughed Bounce. With the leaf as their toboggan, the three bugs sailed over the snowy hills with a *whoosh*.

"*Whoo-hoo!*" cried Miss Spider.

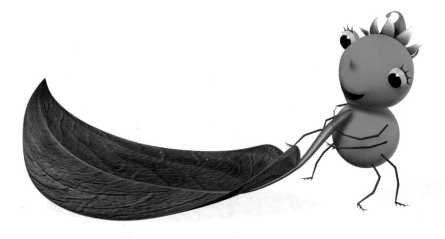

Sliding onto a frozen pond, the toboggan spun out of control.

"Look *ooouuut!*" Squirt shouted. "I can't steer!"

They landed headfirst in a snow bank.

"That was fun!" Bounce giggled, shaking off the snow. "But I'm dizzy!"

The snow fell harder and harder.

"Do you think we'll make it home in time, Mom?" asked Squirt nervously.

Just then, the wind sent Bounce flying through the snowy air. Miss Spider barely managed to catch him before he blew away.

"Never mind home!" she declared with a shiver. "We need to get out of this storm!"

Back at the Cozy Hole, everyone was worried about the missing buggy travelers.

"I wish they were here," Shimmer said sadly. "Holly Day isn't the same without them."

"Holly Day is a time to be jolly," Grandma Betty reminded her. "Let's put some bright red berries all around the door to welcome them when they arrive!"

Miss Spider and her boys were slowly crawling through the storm when a terrible stink filled the air.

Squirt wrinkled his nose. "*Ewww!* What's that smell?" he gasped.

Bounce sniffed into the breeze. "It smells like . . ."

"*Stinky!*" they both cried.

"Come on in and warm your antennae by the fire!" Stinky called as he popped his head out of a hole in the snow.

Outside the wind howled, but inside Stinky's hole it was nice and toasty.

"Have some garlic soup—extra stinky!" he offered. "It's Grandma Smelly's secret recipe!"

"Why Stinky, how thoughtful!" Miss Spider coughed, her eyes watering as she tasted a spoonful. "My, my, it is *quite* strong!"

Everybuggy was quiet after they finished eating. Miss Spider and her boys were no longer cold, but they were still homesick.

"I have an idea!" Stinky said brightly. "Do any of you know the Jolly Holly Day song?"

"We do!" Bounce and Squirt yelled eagerly.

Stinky played his xylophone and they sang the familiar carol. Everybuggy felt cheery again.

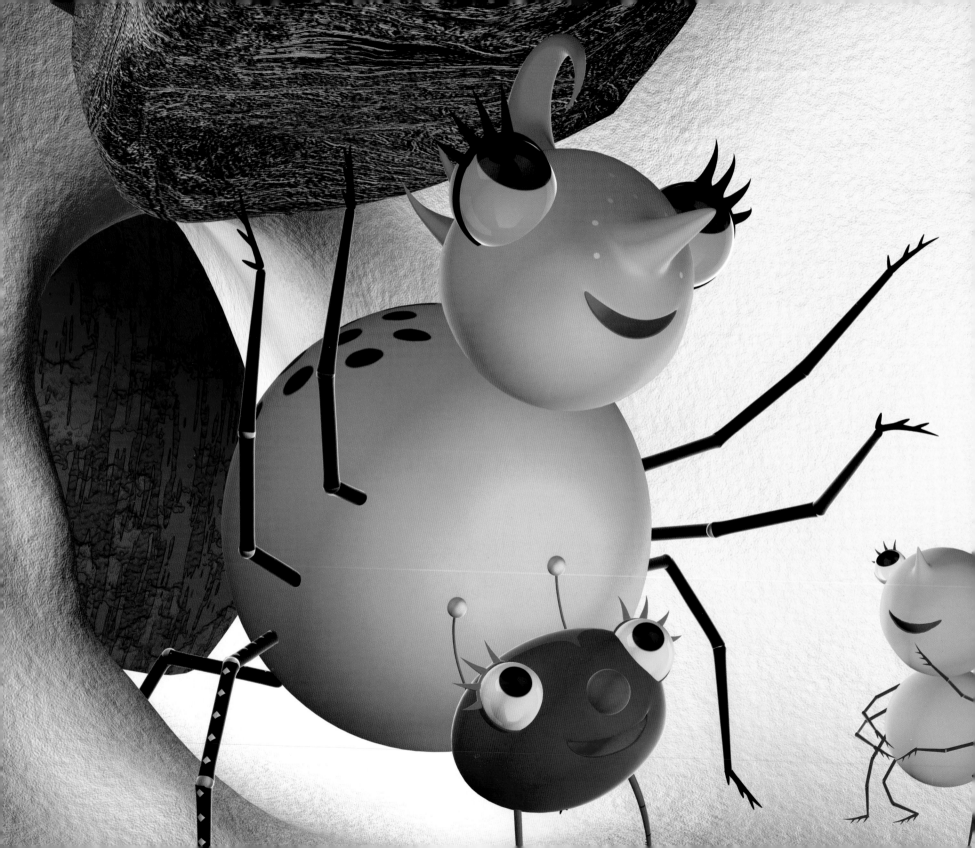

A little while later, the bugs popped their heads outside. The snow had stopped!

"I think we can head out, gang," said Miss Spider.

"Jolly Holly Day, Stinky," Bounce and Squirt called.

"Thank you for taking care of us during the storm," said Miss Spider, giving Stinky the holly berry cake.

The little family was on its way home again. They shivered as the sun sank below the horizon.

"My th-thorax is totally f-frozen!" said Bounce.

"It's too dark to go any further," said Miss Spider sadly. "We'll have to stop here for the night."

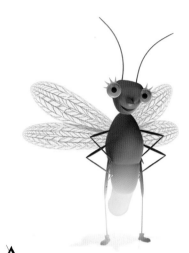

All of a sudden, a faint glow appeared in the night sky, growing brighter as it sparkled through the snow. Flint the Firefly whizzed overhead.

"It's never dark when Flint is here!" he called. "I'll light your way home!"

"Hooray, Flint!" Squirt cheered.

Bounce was so excited that he couldn't stop bouncing.

"Here you are, folks!" said Flint as they arrived at the Cozy Hole.

"Thank you for being our guide, Flint!" Miss Spider said with a big, buggy smile. "Jolly Holly Day!"

Everybuggy exchanged bug hugs as the wanderers climbed into their warm and welcoming Cozy Hole.

"It's so good to be home," Squirt sighed.

"Now we have even more to be jolly about," said Holley. "Let the feasting begin!"

The snug and snuggly bugs sang a joyful song as they gathered 'round the table. This would be their jolliest Holly Day feast of all.

Copyright © 2005 by Callaway & Kirk Company LLC. All rights reserved. Published by Callaway & Kirk Company, a division of Callaway Arts & Entertainment. Miss Spider, Sunny Patch Friends, and all related characters are trademarks and/or registered trademarks of Callaway & Kirk Company LLC, a division of Callaway Arts & Entertainment. Callaway & Kirk Company LLC, Callaway Arts & Entertainment, and their respective logotypes are trademarks and/or registered trademarks. All rights reserved. Digital art by Callaway Animation Studios under the direction of David Kirk in collaboration with Nelvana Limited.

This book is based on the TV episode "Dashing Through the Snow," written by Nadine Van Der Velde and Scott Kraft, from the animated TV series *Miss Spider's Sunny Patch Friends* on Nick Jr., a Nelvana Limited/Absolute Pictures Limited co-production in association with Callaway Arts & Entertainment, based on the Miss Spider books by David Kirk.

Nicholas Callaway, President and Publisher
Cathy Ferrara, Managing Editor and Production Director
Toshiya Masuda, Art Director • Nelson Gomez, Director of Digital Technology
Joya Rajadhyaksha, Associate Editor • Amy Cloud, Associate Editor
Alex Ballas, Assistant Designer • Raphael Shea, Art Assistant • Krupa Jhaveri, Design Assistant
Bill Burg, Digital Artist • Cara Paul, Digital Artist • Aharon Charnov, Digital Artist

Special thanks to the Nelvana staff, including Doug Murphy, Scott Dyer, Tracy Ewing, Pam Lehn,
Tonya Lindo, Mark Picard, Susie Grondin, Luis Lopez, Eric Pentz, and Georgina Robinson.

No part of this publication may be reproduced, or stored in a retrieval system, or transmitted in any form or by any means, electronic, mechanical, photocopying, recording, or otherwise, without written permission of the publisher.

Library of Congress Cataloging-in-Publication Data available upon request.

Distributed in the United States by Viking Children's Books.

Visit Callaway Arts & Entertainment at www.callaway.com.

ISBN 0-448-43998-0

10 9 8 7 6 5 4 3 2   06 07 08 09 10

First edition, September 2005

Printed in China

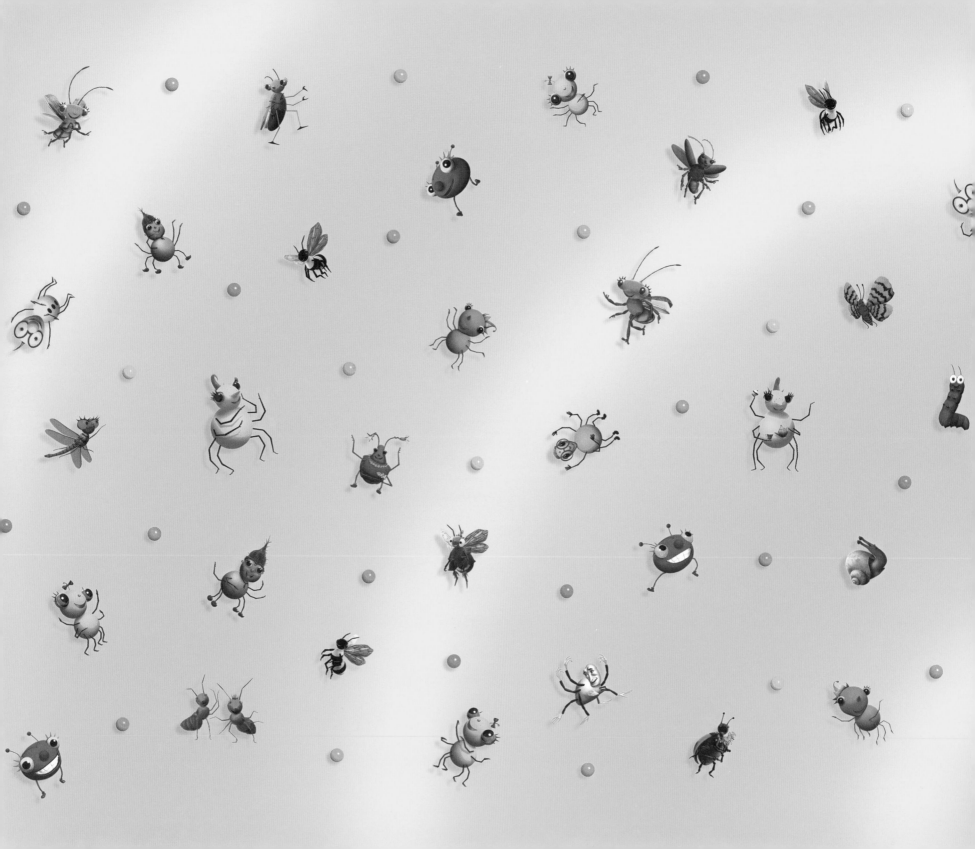